Lands of our Ancestors Book Two

Teacher's Guide

Developed by Dessa Drake
and Gary Robinson

© 2018 Tribal Eye Productions
P.O. Box 1123 / Santa Ynez, CA 93460
www.tribaleyeproductions.com

Lands of our Ancestors Book Two Teacher's Guide
© 2018 Tribal Eye Productions
ISBN 978-0-692-16258-3

TABLE OF CONTENTS

Lands of Our Ancestors Book Two
Teacher's Guide Introduction

This Teacher's Guide is designed to enrich teaching Lands of Our Ancestors Book Two across the curriculum. The guide begins with the California Content Standards for 4th grade History-Social Sciences the book addresses. This information will provide the teacher with important information about what the focus should be in teaching the Mexican Rancho Unit. This is followed by an Overview of the Mexican Rancho period in California history. In addition, there are pages of images of life during the Rancho Era. These images help illustrate the story. At this point the guide also includes a section that validates the accuracy of the events portrayed in the story and a list of sources of further information on the Chumash people and the historic ranchos and adobes.

The eighth section of the guide contains the same "Characters and Relationships" reference as well as the "Timeline" found in the book. Section ten, the largest section of this guide, contains "Questions, Answers, and Words to Know" for each chapter of Book Two. The questions can be used in teacher-directed class discussions, small group discussions, or as written work. The variety of questions in each chapter align with The Six Levels of Questioning: knowledge, comprehension, application, analysis, synthesis, evaluation. Answers are provided for all chapter questions. New vocabulary, including words from the Samala Chumash, Yokuts, and Spanish languages, are found in each chapter's "Words to Know" page.

Finally, to extend the learning after the book is completed, the guide includes possible project choices to engage students. The projects are designed to meet the needs of the diverse learners found in most classrooms. Each project meets a specific fourth grade History-Social Science Content Standard for California Public Schools. The standard is listed with each project.

Students who complete reading the story, discuss or write responses to the questions, and learn the new vocabulary words will meet a variety of the fourth grade California Common Core State Standards in reading, writing, and language.

California Fourth Grade History Social-Science Standards

4.2 Students describe the social, political, cultural, and economic life and interactions among people of California from the pre-Columbian societies to the Spanish mission and Mexican rancho periods.

> 4.2.5: Describe the daily lives of the people, native and nonnative, who occupied the presidios, missions, ranchos, and pueblos.
>
> 4.2.6: Discuss the role of the Franciscans in changing the economy of California from a hunter-gatherer economy to an agricultural economy.
>
> 4.2.7: Describe the effects of the Mexican War for Independence on Alta California, including its effects on the territorial boundaries of North America.
>
> 4.2.8: Discuss the period of Mexican rule in California and its attributes, including land grants, secularization of the missions, and the rise of the rancho economy.

from *https://www.cde.ca.gov/be/st/ss/documents/histsocscistnd.pdf*

We recommend also consulting the California History Social Studies Framework for additional background information. The framework focuses on missions and the rancho period beginning on page 9 of the PDF version found at

https://www.cde.ca.gov/ci/hs/cf/documents/hssfwchapter7.pdf

Overview of the Mexican Rancho Period

Mexico achieved independence from Spain in 1821 and created a functioning republic in 1824. During this time, and for several decades afterwards, the new nation suffered through periods of strife between competing factions vying for very different forms of government. In Mexican California, this instability deeply affected the Indian population at the missions, contributing to the decline of the missions. It was during this time that the most serious mission uprisings occurred.

Contributing to the decline of the missions were the thousands of neophytes who simply fled when conditions became intolerable, as well as the thousands of Indians who died from disease. In 1821, the number of neophytes at the various missions peaked at 21,000, but by 1834, less than 16,000 remained.

In 1833, the Mexican government passed a law that secularized the missions. The law required the missions to give up control over the neophytes and the missions were to be converted into pueblos with lands distributed among the Indians living there. Livestock, equipment and seeds previously belonging to the missions were also supposed to be supplied to the freed neophytes.

However, most of the land and property designated for the ex-neophytes fell into the hands of the Californios and were turned into private estates called ranchos. Many of the Indians were driven off. Some drifted into Mexican towns looking for jobs, while others found work on the ranchos. Still others moved to the interior regions of California hoping to find relatives or fellow tribesmen already living there.

By the mid-1830s, the ranchos were growing and the demand for cheap labor increased. It was the ex-neophytes who flocked to the pueblos and ranchos who filled this demand. Away from the towns, the vast majority of Indians worked for the Californios on ranchos. Although the ranchos were organized to sell products and turn a profit, in reality they produced little marketable goods. Instead, they were basically subsistence institutions, producing only enough to support their Mexican and Indian residents.

Unlike the missions, where all aspects of the lives of the neophytes were strictly regulated, the rancheros were not concerned with the non-economic activities of their Indian workers. Some rancheros allowed families and kin groups to remain intact and community life to continue relatively undisturbed. Even so, the rancheros relegated their Indian workers to a dependency position because the Indians were paid "in kind" and not in cash. The land upon which they built their villages and raised their crops and animals were controlled by the rancheros.

California Indians were economically important to the successful operation of the ranchos as reflected in a statement made by a prominent ranchero:

Many of the rich men of the country had from twenty to sixty Indian servants whom they dressed and fed.... Indians tilled our soil, pastured our cattle, sheared our sheep, cut our lumber, built our houses, paddled our boats, made tiles for our homes, ground our grain, slaughtered our cattle, dressed their hides for market, and made our unburnt bricks; while the Indian women made excellent servants, took good care of our children, made very one of our meals...

-Salvador Vallejo in Cook 1943b:51

Independent Indians from the interior frequently raided coastal ranchos, not to destroy lives or property, but to capture horses. The enormous herds of horses were easy and tempting targets, and the Indians preferred them to cattle as a food source because they were easier to drive off. The animals also fulfilled transportation and trade needs. Indians continually raided the ranchos' horse herds, and this continued well into the 1870s, long after the Americans took over California. By substituting new food sources for those wiped out by Spanish and Mexican settlements, many Indians became heavy consumers of meat. This dietary change saved entire villages from starvation.

As Mexican settlements expanded, the Mexican military, responding to the demands for new laborers, began raiding interior Indian groups for laborers; thus Native resistance began to stiffen. Formerly peaceful, sedentary, localized groups changed to semi-warlike, semi-nomadic groups and began to take the offensive. Adopting guerilla warfare tactics, interior people underwent considerable physical and military adaptation. In the central valley, the Indian offensive reached a peak in 1845; in fact, so successful were Indian raids on coastal settlements that the Mexican government resolved to establish a military border police and erect a fort at Pacheco Pass to prevent further raids.

Mexican authorities and land barons also responded to such raids with punitive expeditions against the interior people, resulting in enslavement of many Indians and acts against them of almost unheard of barbarity. For example, in 1837, José Marí Amador, a wealthy rancher, led a party of civilians, soldiers, and Indian auxiliaries on an expedition into the San Joaquin Valley, where they encountered a group of about 200 suspected wrongdoers, including 100 or so ex-neophytes. Amador wrote that he *"invited the wild Indians and their Christian companions to come and have a feast."* When the Indians came into the Mexican's camp, armed members of the expedition who had been in hiding surrounded the Indians and quickly subdued them. Amador then separated out the Christian Indians and, as he wrote,

At every half-mile or mile, we put six of them on their knees, making them understand that they were about to die. Each one was shot with four arrows, two in front and two in the back. Those who refused to die immediately were killed with spears. On the road were killed in this manner the 100 Christians.

Later Amador decided to execute the unconverted prisoners, after he first baptized them.

I ordered Nazario Galindo to take a bottle of water and I took another. He began at one part of the crowd and I at another. We baptized all the Indians and afterwards they were shot in the back. At the first volley, 70 fell dead. I doubled the charge for the 30 who remained, and they all fell.

Even more devastating to Indians in the Central Valley than such murderous expeditions were the whites' diseases. In the early 1830s, trappers for the Hudson's Bay Company passed through the Great Valley, introducing malaria into the marshy interior lowlands. The disease killed an estimated 20,000 Indians and remained endemic thereafter. By the end of the Mexican occupation, the total Native population of California had been reduced to about 100,000 persons.

Images of Mexican Rancho Life

ABOVE: Example of a two story Mexican Rancho house similar to the one described in Lands of our Ancestors Book Two
-Petaluma Adobe State Historic Park

LEFT: Example of Mexican Rancho map that shows the boundary lines of neighboring ranchos. This map shows ranchos in Alameda County near Hayward.
-Hayward Area Historical Society

RIGHT: Example of work space and storage area inside the first floor of a rancho house like the one described in Lands of our Ancestors Book Two.

Images of Mexican Rancho Life - Page 2

LEFT: Vaquero at work on a Mexican Rancho around 1830. - *Artist unknown. Image in public domain.*

Rancheros and their Brands

Francisco Badillo	Luis Arellanes	Juan Rodriguez
José de la Guerra	Patricio Cota	Antonio Ruiz
Octaviano Gutierrez	Narciso Fabrigat	José Lugo
Juan Camarillo	Juan Cordero	Juan Pico
Refugio Carrillo	José Ortega	Rita Ontiveros
Santa Barbara Mission	Augustin Janssens	Maria Sanchez

RIGHT: Examples of Mexican Rancho cattle brands similar to the one described in <u>Lands of our Ancestors Book Two</u>.

LEFT: Example of a bull and bear fight similar to the one described in <u>Lands of our Ancestors Book Two</u>. These were common forms of entertainment for people of the Mexican Ranchos. *-"Sport in California, A Bull and Bear Fight" by Samuel Waller; Look and Learn/ Bridgeman Images*

Examples of Traditional California Native Structures

Chumash House - Ap (op)

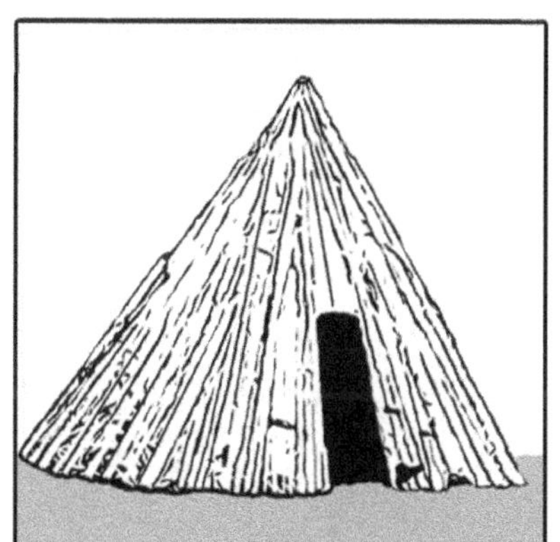

Styles of Yokuts Houses

One Example of Native Sweat House showing underground cutaway. Other similar designs were used by California tribes.

Accuracy of Events Portrayed in <u>Lands of our Ancestors Book Two</u>

This work of historical fiction depicts what <u>might</u> have happened to California Native Americans as Alta California transitioned from Spanish control to Mexican control in the 1820s to 1830s. Although the characters and the specific plot are fictional, the people and events in the book are based on, and taken from, historical documents and the historical writings of non-fiction authors and scholars.

More specifically, for example, many of the details of California rancho life for Native Americans came directly from Stephen W. Silliman's <u>Lost Laborers in Colonial California: Native Americans and the Archaeology of Rancho Petaluma</u>. Silliman's work at Petaluma reveals much about daily life, ranch organization, living and labor conditions, living quarters and annual activities at a California Mexican rancho.

Scenes depicting activities of the vaqueros can be found in multiple historical print and image sources, as can descriptions of the bull and bear fight, which served as entertainment for the regular amusement of the region's Californios.

The battle scenes between Indians and Mexican soldiers depicted in Chapters 12 and 13 of <u>Lands of our Ancestors Book Two</u> are derived from the last three chapters of Elias Castillo's exhaustively researched <u>A Cross of Thorns</u>. That work, in turn, relied on earlier historical works, particularly the anthology <u>Native American Perspectives on the Hispanic Colonization of Alta California</u>, published in 1991, edited by California Native author Edward D. Castillo.

However, in many cases, the way Native Americans were treated during the Mexican Rancho period depended on the nature and beliefs of the *rancheros* (ranch owners) themselves. A few Native *rancho* laborers enjoyed more freedoms and better conditions than those depicted in the <u>Lands of our Ancestors</u> series.

However the period is depicted, the truth is that the Mexican Rancho period contributed heavily to the further destruction and devastation of Native American peoples, communities and cultures in the region that became known as California.

<u>Sources on the Chumash People:</u>

1. <u>California's Chumash Indians,</u> A Project of the Santa Barbara Museum of Natural History; EZ Nature Books; 1992, Revised Edition 2002.
2. <u>The Chumash, Seafarers of the Pacific Coast</u>; Karen Bush Gibson; Capstone Press, 2004.
3. "The Samala People" (DVD); produced by the Santa Ynez Band of Chumash Indians; Available from the tribe's Culture Department; 805-688-7997.
4. <u>Bad Indians: A Tribal Memoir</u>; Deborah A. Miranda; Heyday, 2013.
5. <u>Samala-English Dictionary-A Guide to the Samala Language of the Ineseno Chumash People</u>; Santa Ynez Band of Chumash Indians with Richard Applegate, PhD; 2007.
6. Website: www.sbnature.org/research/anthro/chumash/intro.htm (Chumash section of the Santa Barbara Museum of Natural History's website)
7. Website: www.santaynezchumash.org/history.html (The Santa Ynez Band of Chumash Indians official website)
8. Wikipedia Website: https://en.wikipedia.org/wiki/Chumash_people.

<u>Sources on Mexican Ranchos in California:</u>

1. Silliman, Stephen W. <u>Lost Laborers in Colonial California: Native Americans and the Archaeology of Rancho Petaluma.</u> University of Arizona Press, Tucson, 2004.
2. Castillo, Elias. <u>Cross of Thorns: The Enslavement of California's Indians by the Spanish Missions.</u> Craven Street Books, Fresno, 2015.

3. Timbrook, Jan. <u>Chumash Ethnobotany: Plant Knowledge Among the Chumash People of Southern California</u>. Santa Barbara Museum of Nat'l History, Santa Barbara, 2007.

4. Richard Applegate and the Santa Ynez Chumash Education Committee. <u>Samala-English Dictionary: A Guide to the Samala Language of the Ineseño Chumash People</u>. 2007.

5. John P. Harrington's field notes from Maria Solares, Fernando Librado and other Native California consultants. Available through the J.P. Harrington Database Project located in the Culture Department of the Pechanga Tribe near Temecula, California.

6. Cook, Sherburne F. <u>The Conflict Between the California Indian and White Civilization</u>. University of California Press, 1976.

Characters and Relationships in the <u>Lands of our Ancestors</u> series

Kilik (Miguel) – main character, son of Solomol and Wonono

Tuhuy (Rafael) – Kilik's cousin, son of Salapay and Yol

Stuk (Maria) – Kilik's younger sister

Solomol – Kilik's father

Salapay – Tuhuy's father

Wonono – Kilik's mother

Yol – Tuhuy's mother

Alol-koy – Chumash boy with the children who escaped the mission

Tah-chi – Yokuts Indian scout for the Place of Condors village

Lau-lau – Kilik's first wife

Kai-ina – Kilik's second wife, mother of Malik

Toh-yosh – Lead warrior for the Place of Condors village

Taya – Tuhuy's Chumash wife

Alapay (Andrea) – Tuhuy's daughter and Malik's cousin

Malik (Mateo) – Kilik's son and Andrea's cousin

Mo-Loke – Chumash elder in the Place of Condors village

Diego – Native outlaw and leader of Indians who attacked ranches

Francisco Pacheco – Mexican Ranch owner of *Rancho Caballeros*

Mrs. Pacheco – Ranch owner's wife, mother of Magdalena

Magdalena – Ranch owner's daughter

Esteban - Ranch foreman at *Rancho Caballero*

Pedro – Assistant foreman at *Rancho Caballero*

Timeline of Historical and Fictional Events in
the <u>Lands of our Ancestors</u> series

1769	First Spanish mission established near what is now San Diego
1776	Solomol is born at the Place of River Turtles village
1777	Salapay is born at the Place of River Turtles village
1792	Kilik is born (when Solomol is 16)
1793	Tuhuy is born
1797	Kilik's sister Stuk is born
1804	Kilik & family go to the new mission
1806	The children escape the mission on Summer Solstice morning
	The children arrive at the Place of Condors village
1811	Kilik marries Lau-lau (Yokuts) - Kilik is 19
1812	Dec. 21 - Earthquake damages missions in Chumash territory
	Kilik's unborn baby and wife die the day of the earthquake
1813	Stuk dies from measles brought to the village by visitor
1814	Tuhuy leaves village to live alone, study healing, contact ancestors
	Kilik leaves village to explore the region and to raid
	missions and ranches
1819	Kilik returns to village, meets Kai-ina (Yokuts woman)
	Tuhuy returns to village, sees Taya (Coastal Chumash)
1820	Tuhuy marries Taya - Tuhuy is 27
	Simultaneous wedding ceremony: Kilik marries Kai-ina
1821	Malik is born to Kilik (who is 29 years old) & Kai-ina
	Mexico wins independence from Spain
1822	Alapay is born to Tuhuy and Taya
1823+	Cousins Malik and Alapay grow and play together
1824	Kilik begins raiding ranches and missions for cattle - age 32

1825-30	Alapay blends healing and fighting as needed
1832	Kilik turns 40 years old
1833	Tuhuy turns 40 years old
1833	Kilik trains Malik as hunter & warrior
	Alapay learns hunting and fighting skills as well
	Spanish padres expelled from missions - Mission Indians released
	Francisco Pacheco gets major land grant - needs laborers
	Epidemic outbreak (flu or malaria)
1834-1848	Major Mexican *Rancho* Period
1834	Kilik finds crippled father, brings him and aunt Yol back
	Pacheco's men raid Condor Village; take Tuhuy and others to *Rancho Caballeros*
	Tuhuy and everyone held at ranch, must work
	Kilik raids Rancho Caballero, rescues family

Chapter Questions & Answers

Words to Know

Chapter 1 - Survival Skills
Questions

1. Describe the main characters Kilik and Tuhuy. In what ways are they the same characters from Book One?

2. Summarize this chapter. What exactly are Kilik and Tuhuy doing and why?

3. List some steps the children take to keep from getting caught.

4. Based on what occurs in this chapter, do you think Salapay and Solomol were right to place such a responsibility on their young sons? Cite evidence to explain your reasoning.

Chapter 1
Answers

1. Kilik is 14 years old. He is still very much a leader. He is skilled at hunting.

   Tuhuy is 13 years old. He is still very much a thinker. He remembers the words of his elders.

   The boys still work together well.

2. Kilik and Tuhuy are in the midst of an escape from the mission. Although Kilik was put in charge by his father, both boys are trying to help a small group of children reach Sacred Mountain and hopefully, freedom.

3. They choose a hidden spot near a creek to camp, they stay off of the main trails, and they are aware of whether or not it is safe to build a fire.

4. Answers may vary, but evidence cited might include: Alol-koy trusts the two as leaders; the boys have successfully brought the children this far, keeping them off the trails and providing them with food.

Chapter 1
Words to Know

<u>Chumash Names and Words</u>:

Kilik (K<u>ee</u>-leek): Sparrow Hawk; teenage boy
Tuhuy (Too-<u>hooy</u>): Rain; teenage boy, Kilik's cousin
Stuk (Rhymes with Luke): Ladybug; Kilik's sister
Alol-koy: Dolphin; boy with the children who escaped the mission

Words to Know
(in order of appearance in the story)

elder: a respectful term for those older than you in a tribe

shackles: U-shaped fastening devices secured by bolts that confine
the legs or arms

Summer Solstice: the longest day of the year, when Grandfather Sun's
power is strongest

quiver: a case for holding arrows, usually made from animal skin

Chapter 2 - The Village that Ran Away
Questions

1. What evidence from this chapter supports what we already know about the personalities of Kilik and Tuhuy?

2. Describe the Place of Condors. Why is it not like a typical Native village?

3. In this chapter, there is some foreshadowing about the futures of Kilik and Tuhuy, two boys who share a strong bond and whose paths have thus far been closely linked. What does it appear may lie ahead for these two cousins?

Chapter 2
Answers

1. Kilik, as a leader and boy of action, pokes around the abandoned village. He is eager to get the children safely to the new village. He takes to riding and working with the horses well.

   Tuhuy, the thinker, comforts the children. He wants to offer prayers up on Sacred Mountain. He increases his knowledge by learning how to plant crops and grow food.

2. The village has different housing: traditional Chumash dwellings and traditional Yokut dwellings. There is also a ceremonial area, playing field, and granary. Crops are being grown. Horses are corralled there. This is not a village of one tribe; it is a village of people from several tribes, survivors of the missions. They do not speak the same traditional languages or ways of living, but their experiences with the Spanish are the same. They are combining all of this in order to survive in this land that is not the same as it was before the Spanish arrived.

3. Tuhuy mentions a couple of times that he and his cousin may begin leading different paths. Kilik appears to be following the path of the warrior, whereas Tuhuy has been noticed by the elders as one who may become a healer and spiritual leader.

Chapter 2
Words to Know

<u>Yokuts Names</u>:

Tah-chi: Yokut scout given the name of his tribe as a nickname; guides the children to the Place of Condors

Toh-yosh: Arrow; leads the warriors of the Place of Condors

Words to Know
(in order of appearance in the story)

approached: came nearer to

tule reeds: tall, green reeds with spongy stems

uprising: an act of resistance or rebellion; a revolt

emerge: to become known or apparent

Chapter 3 - Starting Over
Questions

1. When Kilik is sixteen and ventures out alone to search for his parents, an unexpected event occurs. What does this event demonstrate about him?

2. Kilik and Tuhuy's separate paths further develop in this chapter. Using a graphic organizer, map out the sequence of events for each character.

3. Do you agree with the way Kilik decided to deal with the loss of his wife, unborn child, and sister? Explain your reasoning.

Chapter 3
Answers

1. Kilik is brave, but sometimes acts without thinking things through. He is smart, however; he did not lead the soldiers to the Place of Condors. His bravery and skill are tested and proven. He does not yet have the capability to kill another human being.

2. Kilik:

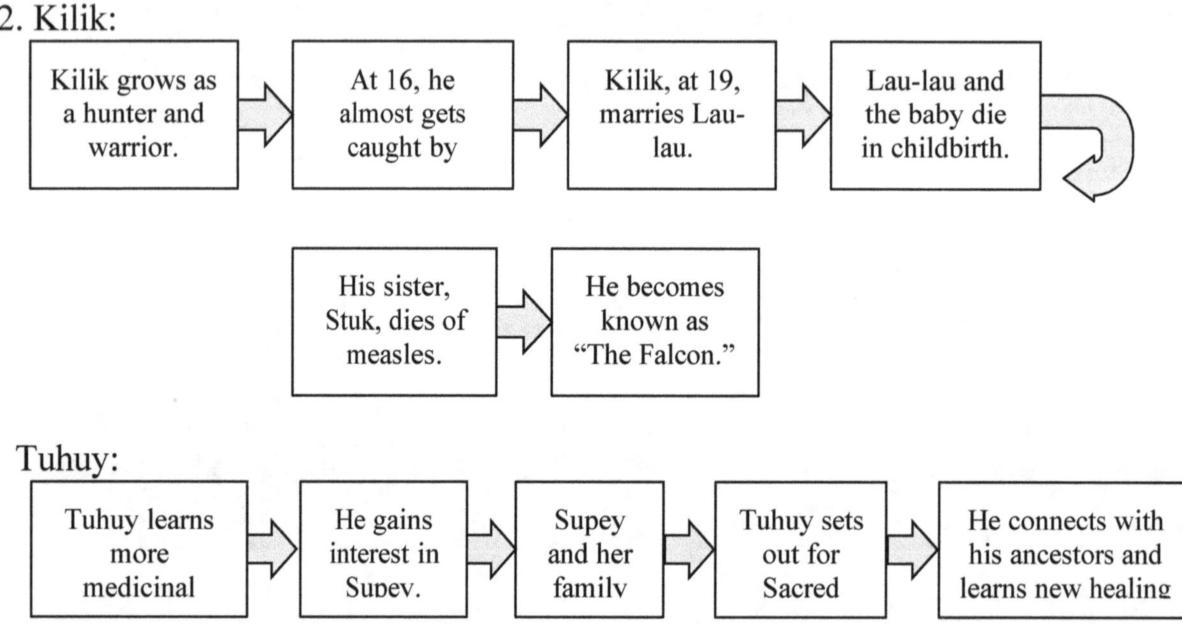

Tuhuy:

3. Student answers will vary.

**Chapter 3
Words to Know**

<u>Yokuts Name:</u>

Lau-lau: Butterfly; Kilik's wife

<u>Samala Chumash Name:</u>

Supey: Ornament or adornment; Tuhuy's love interest

**Chapter 3
Words to Know
(in order of appearance in the story)**

malnutrition: lack of proper nutrition, caused by not having enough to eat, not eating enough of the right things, or being unable to use the food that one does eat

commandant: an officer in charge of a particular unit

hobbled: tied or strapped together to prevent escape

Winter Solstice: the shortest day of the year

honed: refined or perfected

notoriety: the state of being famous or well known for some bad quality or deed

Chapter 4 - New Generations
Questions

1. What historical event is referred to in this chapter?

2. Other events occur that affect or have the potential to affect Native people in California in this chapter. What are they?

3. Why do Kilik and Tuhuy give their children Spanish names? Why were they hesitant to do so?

Chapter 4
Answers

1. Mexico gains independence from Spain in 1821 and thus, control over Alta California.

2. Spanish colonizers are building towns and ranches throughout California. The traditional plants and herbs gathered by Native people are disappearing, as are the animals they would traditionally hunt. There is a drought.

3. Kilik and Tuhuy give their children Spanish names in case of future interactions with Californios or Mexican authorities, and also to protect them from those who might do them harm. The men are hesitant to give their children Spanish names because they want to maintain their Chumash traditions, not carry on a practice of the Spanish invaders.

Chapter 4
Words to Know

<u>Yokuts Names and Words</u>:

Kai-ina: Kilik's second Yokut wife

<u>Chumash Names</u>:

Taya: Abalone; Tuhuy's Chumash wife

Malik: First-Born Child; Kilik's son

Koko: Samala for "father"

Alapay: Above; Tuhuy's daughter

Words to Know
(in order of appearance in the story)

reunited: came together again after a period of separation

remote: far from the main centers of population

reluctantly: in an unwilling and hesitant way

cautious: careful to avoid potential problems or dangers

persevered: continued on despite facing difficulties or little chance of success

tumultuous: confusing, disorderly

Chapter 5 - More of the Same
Questions

1. Describe how each of the three historical events taking place in this chapter affected the Native people of California.

2. Contrast the European perspective of land with that of Native people. Which do you think is better, and why?

3. What details about a *rancho* do you learn from this chapter?

4. The characters in this book suffer repeated loss and tragedy, the knowledge of which is evident particularly in this chapter. What feelings would you have experienced if you were Kilik, upon learning of these additional losses? If you were Solomol? What do you think motivates them to keep going despite all of these hardships?

Chapter 5
Answers

1. The flu epidemic of 1833 caused thousands of deaths among Native people because they had no immunity or traditional medicines prepared to deal with this illness that came from Europeans.

The closing of the missions in 1833 was supposed to return land to Native people, but few received any. Most had no home and no way to sustain themselves once the missions closed.

The creation of large *ranchos* from the giving away of land grants created the need for a labor force. *Rancheros* like Francisco Pacheco used former mission Indians to fulfill this need.

2. Europeans believed in land ownership and divided up land for this purpose. This concept did not exist in Native California. Native people traditionally believed the land was given by Creator for all people. Opinions will vary, but should include reasoning.

3. *Ranchos* developed as a result of land grants being given to Californios by the Mexican government. Hundreds of them were given away. These land grants included thousands of acres of land, primarily for the purpose of raising cattle. Native people, mostly those that once lived and worked within the mission system, served as the labor force on the ranchos. Some of these Native laborers came willingly because they had nowhere else to go, but others were captured, much as they were during the mission period.

4. Answers will vary, but feelings may include grief, despair, anger, shock, sadness, loss of hope, a desire for revenge. Sources of motivation may be the love they have for their family, the survival of the tribe, the desire to see their children or grandchildren grow up, the desire to return to their homeland, or the refusal to allow the invaders to change their lifeways.

Chapter 5
Words to Know

<u>Chumash Words</u>:

'Unu: grandson

Mo-loke: ancient/long ago; elder left behind at the Place of Condors

Words to Know
(in order of appearance in the story)

epidemic: a widespread occurrence of an infectious disease in a community at a particular time

ailment: a minor illness

expelled: forced to leave a place

land grant: a piece of land given by the Mexican government to Mexican citizens

abandoned: deserted

rancho: a cattle ranch

rations: a fixed amount of a commodity, such as food

vaqueros: cowboys; horse-mounted ranch hands

capable: able

vaguely: in a way that is uncertain or unclear

familiar: well known or recognizable

smoldering: burning slowly with smoke, but no flame

Chapter 6 - Kidnapped
Questions

1. Compare and contrast mission life and *rancho* life for Native laborers, using this chapter (and previous chapters) and your own prior knowledge.

2. Do you think Tuhuy's action at *Rancho Caballero* was wise? Why or why not?

3. If you were among those in this kidnapped group, how would you be feeling as you arrive at this rancho and observe and listen to what's in store for you?

Chapter 6
Answers

1. Like the missions, many of the buildings on a *rancho* were made of adobe bricks. Also, Native people did much/all of the labor. They received food, clothing, and a place to sleep in exchange for their labor. The main house of a rancho, like a mission, was typically built in the quadrangle formation, with a central courtyard. Indian servants tended to the needs of the *ranchero's* family much as they would the padres of a mission. Similar to the missions, Indian laborers produced several products on *ranchos*, including saddles, boots, rugs, candles, and blankets.

   Unlike the missions, families were not separated from each other on the *ranchos*. The focus of the *rancho* was cattle, so *vaqueros* were workers on ranchos that were not at the missions. This required many horses on a *rancho*, which was not necessary at a mission. A *rancho* included a main house that had two levels. The *ranchero* owned a *rancho*, whereas a mission was owned by the Spanish government and run by Spanish Catholic padres.

2. Answers may vary and may include: it was risky for Tuhuy to put himself in such a prominent position, because he will be blamed if anything goes wrong; or that it was wise to try to control how the rest of the Native laborers will be treated and where the people you care about will be placed within the rancho labor system.

3. Student responses will vary.

Chapter 6
Words to Know
(in order of appearance in the story)

whimpered: made low, feeble sounds expressing fear, pain, or discontent

skirted: went around or passed the edge of

trek: a long, arduous journey, especially one made on foot

vowed: promised

vast: immense; of very great extent or quantity

ranchero: the owner of a rancho

addressing: speaking to another person or group of people, usually in a formal way

dormitories: rooms in which several people sleep

simultaneously: at the same time

foreman: a worker who supervises and directs other workers

jefecito indio: "little Indian boss" - supervisor of the Indians

Chapter 7 – Vaqueros and Maid Servants
Questions

1. The job of *vaquero* was vital to rancho life. Describe the tasks and skills required of a *vaquero*.

2. In this chapter, Malik and Alapay become conflicted as they learn and master their new tasks on the *rancho*. Why are they conflicted? Explain an instance in which you have had conflicting thoughts.

Chapter 7
Answers

1. *Vaqueros* are skilled at:
   - riding a horse
   - creating and controlling a *reata* or lariat
   - roping and tying a calf or steer
   - rounding up and herding cattle
   - separating cattle
   - branding cattle

2. Malik is conflicted because he is proud to be successfully learning the skills of a *vaquero*; yet, these skills largely represent the culture Malik knows his father and uncle despise.

Alapay is conflicted because she has found an ally of sorts in Magdalena, the *ranchero's* daughter. As nice as Magdalena may be to her, Alapay knows she is merely a servant and that the other members of Magdalena's family do not share such a compassionate view of her or the other servants.

Student answers to personal experience will vary.

Chapter 7
Words to Know
(in order of appearance in the story)

trustee: a person who works for those in charge (in this case, the padres of the mission) and makes sure rules are followed

fortified: strengthened with defenses in order to prevent attack

forbidden: not allowed

Indio Jefe: another Spanish term for "boss of the Indians"

lasso: also known as a *reata* or lariat; a rope with a noose at one end

steer: a neutered bovine male

eased: made something unpleasant less serious or severe

domestic: related to family or the running of a home

robust: strong and healthy

tyrant: a cruel and oppressive ruler

tedious: too long, slow, or dull; tiresome

compassion: sympathy, pity, and concern for the suffering or misfortune of others

inferior: lower in rank, status, or quality

condemnation: very strong disapproval

racial identity: a group of people who share a common history, nationality, or geographic area

Chapter 8 – The *Ranchero's* Daughter
Questions

1. If you were Diego, would you have agreed to help Kilik? Why or why not? What do you think motivated Diego to help him?

2. One may argue that some unethical (wrong, unfair) events take place in this chapter. Describe one of them and explain in what way(s) the event is unethical.

3. What evidence from this chapter supports the inference that Alapay is becoming as good a healer as her father?

Chapter 8
Answers

1. Student answers will vary, but may include the fact that the men have some similarities, in that both are considered outlaws. As a leader of a village of runaways, one might infer that Diego has just as much hatred for the invaders as Kilik does.

2. Student answers may include:
   - Señora Pacheco's treatment of Alapay; the woman made references to Alapay being uncivilized, a dirty Indian, and the reason why her daughter was sick.
   - The spirit of the land's choice to make Magdalena ill; she is an innocent child and treats the Native laborers nicely. She is not the reason why people suffer on this particular *rancho*.

3. Alapay is able to communicate with the spirits of illness and the spirits of the plants. She is able to identify the right plants to use as medicine. Although she has helped her father heal others in the past, she is able to heal Magdalena completely on her own.

Chapter 8
Words to Know
(in order of appearance in the story)

fortifications: defensive walls or other reinforcements built to strengthen a place against attack

irrelevant: not connected, applicable, or pertinent

summoned: urgently demanded for help

civilized: polite and well mannered

whisked: taken away suddenly and quickly

engulfed: surrounded or covered completely by (usually a natural force)

desecrate: to treat a sacred place or thing with violent disrespect

impact: to have a strong effect on someone or something

scurried: moved hurriedly with short, quick steps

agony: extreme physical or mental suffering

meditative: involving meditation or concentrated thought

reverently: with deep and solemn respect

dramatically: greatly

Chapter 9 – The Bear and the Bull
Questions

1. If you were Malik, how would you have dealt with the unethical treatment of the bear?

2. What do Malik's actions in this chapter tell you about his character? In what way(s) is he similar to his father, Kilik?

Chapter 9
Answers

1. Student answers will vary.

2. Student answers will vary, but may include: Malik cares about animals; he believes, as the Chumash do, that bears should be honored and respected. So, like his father, he follows traditional Chumash ways. He knows the bear song and uses it as Kilik once did. He also appears to sometimes act without thinking, as Kilik did when he was younger.

Chapter 9
Words to Know
(in order of appearance in the story)

ignorant: uneducated or unsophisticated

savage: a primitive and uncivilized person; considered a negative term for
Native people

pivoting: spinning or rotating

bellowing: emitting a deep, loud roar

gruesome: causing horror

Indio tonto: Spanish for "Indian fool"

gawkers: people who stare openly at something or someone

tormented: experienced severe mental and/or physical suffering

timidly: shyly; in a way that shows lack of courage or confidence

sauntered: walked in a slow, relaxed manner, without hurry or effort

Que tonto eres: Spanish for "What a fool you are."

predicament: a difficult, unpleasant, or embarrassing situation

Vamonos, muchachos: Spanish for "Let's go, boys."

defy: to openly resist or refuse to obey

Chapter 10 – The Fiesta
Questions

1. Magdalena's parents make their opinions regarding her actions quite clear in this chapter. What is your point of view of Magdalena's behavior? What do her actions say about her character?

2. Tuhuy had to make a quick, difficult decision in this chapter. Do you think he made the right choice? What choice would you have made? Explain your reasoning.

3. Predict what Alapay will do next. What skills and character traits does she have that will assist her?

Chapter 10
Answers

1. Student answers will vary but may include that Magdalena is brave to stand up for Malik and Tuhuy in front of her parents and all of their guests; she is foolish to think she can have any influence over her father.

2. Student answers will vary but may include that Tuhuy made the right decision because it would not have been right to hurt his own nephew; or Tuhuy made the wrong decision because he perhaps could have controlled the level of pain with which Malik had to suffer, and instead they both had to suffer at the hands of a cruel man.

3. Student predictions will vary but should include that Alapay has been taught by her uncle how to hunt and fight, and she also knows how to heal with plants. She knows the Samala Chumash language as well as some Spanish. She is kind and caring, as she took care of Magdalena; yet she is also determined.

Chapter 10
Words to Know
(in order of appearance in the story)

peasant: a poor person of low social status

garb: clothing or dress

devised: planned

sumptuous: splendid

acquaintances: people one knows only slightly, and who are not close friends

barbaric: savagely cruel; exceedingly brutal

spectators: people who watch an event

spectacle: something on display as unusual, notable, or entertaining

anticipation: a feeling of excitement about something that is going to happen

preposterous: utterly absurd or ridiculous

heathen: a term for someone who does not belong to a religion (usually a
negative term)

sternly: in a serious or severe manner

sear: to burn (in this case, a figure of speech)

Chapter 11 – Free at Last
Questions

1. Where might 200 warriors have come from to assist Diego and Kilik in the attack?

2. Kilik has never been one afraid to take risks. Was it wise to sneak onto the rancho prior to the attack? Explain your reasoning. Was it wise to trust the first man Kilik approached with the attack plan? Explain your reasoning.

3. What does it mean for someone to do something "with a gleam in his eye"?

4. Malik and Tuhuy were in a well-guarded room. How do you think it came to be that they were released?

Chapter 11
Answers

1. Student answers will vary, but may include that the warriors were just like Kilik and Diego - former mission Indians who were able to avoid being captured and taken to a *rancho*, or had escaped. Some may have had family at that *rancho* and wanted revenge and/or to help their own families escape.

2. Student answers will vary, but may include that both acts were risky, yet paid off in the long run. Without his visit, the Natives would not have known what was happening and would not have been prepared in advance to assist in the fight. The man he approached could have told Esteban or Señor Pacheco, which would have ruined the plan and possibly hurt his family further; but instead, it helped to prepare the workers and gave Kilik valuable information, like where his son and cousin were being kept.

3. "With a gleam in his/her eye" is an idiom that describes a person's facial expression when he/she is happy, amused, or knows a secret.

4. Accept reasonable responses.

Chapter 11
Words to Know
(in order of appearance in the story)

potentially: with the possibility to develop or happen in the future

detected: discovered or identified

exploits: bold or daring feats

elated: extremely happy

envisioned: imagined; visualized

avenge: to inflict harm in return for injury or wrong against another

unjust: unfair

deliverance: the action of being rescued or set free

silhouetted: shown as a dark shape outlined against a lighter background

barrage: a concentrated artillery bombardment over a wide area

lunged: made a sudden forward movement with the body or a weapon

toppled: became unsteady and fell

ceased: stopped

clenched: pressed tightly together in anger, determination, or to suppress a
strong emotion

Chapter 12 – The *Ranchero's* Revenge
Questions

1. Was it ethical for the Native laborers and servants to take the horses and all the food and tools they could when they left *Rancho Caballero*? Why or why not?

2. Summarize the events that take place once the Natives arrive at the Hidden Place.

3. If you were a former laborer or servant at *Rancho Caballero,* what would your mood be upon arriving at the Hidden Place? What might you say to Diego or Kilik?

4. Why do you suppose Diego and Kilik stayed at the Hidden Place and prepared for another battle instead of leading everyone in the village to another place of safety?

5. This chapter is entitled "The *Ranchero's* Revenge." What event takes place that proves this to be true? If you were Señor Pacheco, would your need for revenge be satisfied? What would be your next move?

Chapter 12
Answers

1. Student answers will vary, but may include that it was unethical because it is wrong to take what does not belong to you; it was ethical because Señor Pacheco never paid his servants or laborers for the work they did on his *rancho* even though he had promised to do so.

2. Events should be similar to:
   - Alapay doctors Malik and Tuhuy
   - Kilik brings the survivors from the Place of Condors to the Hidden Place
   - What remains of Kilik and Tuhuy's families reunite
   - Mexican troops arrive, fight, and retreat
   - Repairs and reinforcements are made to the fortifications
   - Alapay heals Tuhuy in the sweathouse
   - Tuhuy and Kilik reconnect

3. Student answers will vary, but may include relief, happiness, anxious anticipation, or even sadness and anger if he/she was injured or lost a loved one upon leaving the rancho. Accept reasonable, thoughtful responses to the second question.

4. Student answers will vary, but may include that Kilik knew his son and cousin had not healed enough for further travel; Diego and Kilik were confident that their preparations were sufficient to survive and succeed another attack; Diego and Kilik wanted their own revenge.

5. The Mexican troops arriving to attack and kill the Natives were to be Señor Pacheco's revenge. Since they retreated, students may respond that Señor Pacheco will not be satisfied and will indeed send more troops next time. Accept reasonable responses.

Chapter 12
Words to Know
(in order of appearance in the story)

obtain: get, acquire, or secure

seized: took hold of suddenly and forcibly

impending: about to happen

siege: a military operation in which enemy forces surround an area and cut off supplies, in the hopes to force the surrender of those inside

caravan: a group of people traveling together

wielded: held and used

Chapter 13 – The Final Showdown
Questions

1. What character traits might you add to your description of Alapay after her actions in this chapter? Support your answer with evidence.

2. Provide some reasons why, as a Native person, one might fight *with* the Mexican troops instead of against them, besides wanting to be on the "winning side."

3. Compare and contrast the feelings of the Mexican troops with those of the Native warriors in this "final showdown." Include the causes for each of the different feelings you list.

Chapter 13
Answers

1. Students answers will vary, but may include that Alapay is brave to go into battle not only once, but twice; she is a bit reckless for calling out and letting the enemy know where she was hiding (perhaps taking after her uncle a bit); she is a skilled warrior, as she succeeded in wounding the enemy and not getting hurt herself.

2. Student answers will vary, but may include that perhaps the Native person has lost his/her entire family and/or has no village to return to; the *ranchero* for whom he/she works is kind and treats him/her well; he/she was offered a good reward for agreeing to fight against these "rebels"; he/she was forced to fight against them.

3. The Mexican troops as well as the Native warriors may have felt confident, scared, nervous, anxious, or worried at the beginning before the battle started, not knowing what the outcome would be for themselves or their side. The Mexican troops may have started feeling frustrated or shocked when they found that the Native warriors were so well prepared and appeared to be fighting with the sort of military tactics with which they were trained. This may have turned into fear, disappointment, or anger as the Mexican troops

recognized defeat and had to retreat. The Native warriors may have felt pride, elation, and relief as they realized they won, and later sadness and grief if they found they had lost a loved one or friend in the battle.

Chapter 13
Words to Know
(in order of appearance in the story)

adrenaline: a hormone released in your body in times of stress, causing increased breathing and blood flow

contingent: a group of people

platoon: a group of soldiers usually led by a lieutenant

projectiles: objects propelled through the air, usually thrown as weapons

maneuvers: movements requiring skill (in this case military) and care

renegades: people who behave in rebellious, unexpected ways

bugle: a brass instrument like a small trumpet without keys, used for military signals

Chapter 14 – An Uncertain Future
Questions

1. Why are Solomol's use of the phrases "The flood gates have been thrown wide open" and "...ocean of strangers" good ways to describe the manner in which Europeans arrived onto the land now known as California?

2. Do you agree with the choice this family has made? Why or why not?

3. Can you predict the outcome of the journey they have chosen to take? What do you think will happen to the Native people staying behind at the Hidden Place?

4. What makes the events in this story important to California history? Use information from the story and your unit of study to explain your answer.

Chapter 14
Answers

1. When real floodgates open, there's no stopping the rush of water that comes through, much like there was no stopping the arrival of Europeans onto Native land in California and elsewhere in North America. An ocean is vast and hard to measure, much like the numbers of Europeans arriving on the continent during this family's life time.

2. Student opinions will vary, but should include good reasoning.

3. Predictions will vary. Encourage students to use evidence from the text and their own knowledge of the rancho period and California history to make reasonable predictions and support their answers.

4. Student opinions will vary, but may include that the events mark the transition of control over the lands in California from the Spanish to Mexican governments, the continuing and lasting effects of the mission system and Spanish colonizers on the land and Native people (disease, loss of language,

loss of traditional plant and animal resources, land acquisition), the continuance of many of these practices under Mexican control, the destruction of Native culture (or at least the necessity to hide it in order to survive).

Chapter 14
Words to Know
(in order of appearance in story)

lurked: waited in a hidden or distant place in order to do something harmful (used figuratively in this case)

temporary: lasting for a limited period of time; not permanent

inconvenience: a disruption to one's comfort

staunch: loyal and committed

descendants: people descended from a particular ancestor

nestled: situated in a half-hidden position

conflict: a serious disagreement or argument

Lands of Our Ancestors Book Two
Projects

The following suggested projects and activities will extend the learning of early California history across the curriculum. Each project meets at least one of the fourth grade History-Social Science Content Standards in section 4.2:

"Students describe the social, political, cultural, and economic life and interactions among people of California from the pre-Columbian societies to the Spanish mission and Mexican rancho periods."

The projects are appropriate for individual students, partners, or small groups. Completed projects can be presented to the entire class for shared learning. All materials needed for the projects are basic classroom and school supplies. Laptops, notebooks, and the school library are resources the students will also need.

Projects and Activities

Recording History (Standards 4.2.5 and 4.2.8)

Primary sources are important resources to use when researching the past. In this activity, the student(s) will imagine that he/she is living in the 1800s and has been sent by the Mexican government to visit several prominent ranchos and record the sights and sounds of California.

Journal Project: The student(s) will:
- write journal entries, using appropriate dates, describing what he/she sees, eats, how he/she travels, his/her impressions of the ranchos, and the people he/she meets.
- describe the relationships among the rancheros, vaqueros or soldiers, and Native people.
- include drawings of rancho life
- use previous knowledge and new research to complete the project.

Materials: Paper, pencils, markers, colored pencils, laptops, copy of the story, resource books

Timeline Project: The student(s) will:
- create a timeline of the book from the escape to the journey out of the Hidden Place
- use resources to research important facts and dates to post on the timeline.
- use drawings, photos, or other pictures to illustrate the timeline.
- display the timeline in the classroom.

Materials: Butcher paper, colored pencils, markers, paints, glue, laptop, copy of the story, resource books

The Land (Standards 4.2.5, 4.2.6, 4.2.8)

The respect that the Native people in <u>Lands of Our Ancestors</u> have for the land continues in Book 2 despite continued loss of access to their traditional homelands. Throughout this book, several locations become new, temporary homes for the main characters.

Map Project: The student(s) will use the information from the story to create detailed visual representations of each of the following settings, including annotations on post-its or index cards which describe the significance of each part of the visual representation to the story:

- The Place of Condors (map or drawing)
- Rancho Caballero (diseño*)
- The Hidden Place (map or drawing)

Materials: Large construction paper or butcher paper, post-its or index cards, markers, colored pencils, paints, copies of the story

Note: a diseño is a map of the land required by the Mexican government in order to acquire a land grant; images are available in most social studies curricula and can also be found on the internet under "rancho diseño."

Acquiring Knowledge (Standards 4.2.5, 4.2.7, 4.2.8)

Fact Box Project: This game activity reinforces new material learned in the unit of study and will motivate students to research additional information.

The student(s) will cover and decorate a shoe box or similar size box. Decorations should illustrate one of the story themes or scenes. There should be an opening at the top of the box large enough to reach inside. Using index cards, the student will write 15 or more question cards about daily life for Native and non-Native people on the *ranchos*. Answers to the questions should be written on the back of the question cards. Questions can be true or false.

Examples:

Q: Who made the adobe bricks for the rancho buildings?
A: The Native men and boys made the adobe bricks.

Q: True or False? Missions and ranchos had the same purpose.
A: False

Students can play the game one-on-one or in teams, taking turns choosing cards from the box. Students can decide if they want to keep score; awarding points for correct answers or even designating different point values per question based on the difficulty of each.

Materials: Shoe box, paper, scissors, tape, colored pencils, markers, index cards, laptop, resource books, copy of story

Compare and Contrast (Standard 4.2.5)

Poster Project: Student(s) will make three posters to be displayed side by side. Each poster will represent a different group: Natives, *vaqueros*, and soldiers. Students will use words and pictures to illustrate each group's daily life. The side by side display will illustrate the contrast. This project can include an oral presentation or explanation of the information in the posters and students' opinions.

Materials: Poster board, markers, colored pencils, drawings or pictures, glue, laptop, resource books, copy of story

Plants and Animals (Standard 4.2.6, 4.2.7, 4.2.8)

Many of the plants and animals native to the area known as Alta California became threatened when Europeans arrived in large numbers and brought animals and seeds with them. In fact, there is evidence of non-native, otherwise known as invasive, plants within the old adobe bricks used to build the missions. These invasive plants forever changed the hunting and gathering traditions of California Native peoples and thus, their diet, their medicines, their traditions, their culture. Further destruction of the land continued through the establishment of mission agriculture and later, the ranchos.

Mini Display Board Project

Student(s) will research native plants and animals and how they were traditionally used by California Native peoples. Student(s) will also research the invasive plants and animals brought by Europeans and how these non-native species affected the land and Native people who depended on it.

The Mini Display Board will be created using file folders and post-its, allowing the student(s) to include information both on and underneath each post-it. The format may be by the categories listed above, using a compare and contrast organizational structure, or, if research lends itself, using a cause and effect or food chain organizational structure.

Suggested native plants: dogbane, tule, willow, juncus, oak, elderberry, deergrass, yucca, agave, sage, milkweed, sumac, yerba mansa, soap root, manzanita, toyon

Suggested native animals: deer, tule elk, grizzly bear, rabbit, coyote, bobcat, birds of various kinds, mountain lion

Suggested invasive plants: barley, ryegrass, wild oats, curly dock, wild lettuce, wild mustard, spiny sowthistle, redstem filaree (all found in mission adobe bricks) (*students may also consider researching the effect of agriculture on native plants, ie. the vineyards, orchards, and crops like wheat, barley, corn, beans, and peas that were first grown in the missions*)

Suggested invasive animals: horses, cattle, sheep, goats, hogs

Materials: file folders, post-its, pencils, markers, colored pencils, pictures or drawings, laptops, copy of the story, resource books